Kane's Big Picture

An Early intro to Entrepreneurship for Kids

Michael Fernandez Jr.

ISBN: 9781708882037

Kane loves sketching,
drawing and painting.
There was nothing else
he found more entertaining!

HE WOULD SKETCH GIRAFFES ON ROLLERBLADES,
DRAW LITTLE RED LIZARDS.
HE WAS REALLY GREAT AT PAINTING
LEFT-HANDED WIZARDS.

At the beach or the park,
anywhere he would go,
whether Kane was drawing or painting,
he was putting on a show!

KANE WAS USUALLY GOOD IN CLASS,
BUT ONE DAY HE GOT INTO TROUBLE.
INSTEAD OF PAYING ATTENTION,
HE DREW AN ALLIGATOR BLOWING BUBBLES.

KANE TOLD HIS MOMMY AND DADDY,
"I PROMISE TO FOCUS IN CLASS,
IT'S MY FIRST TIME GETTING INTO TROUBLE,
BUT ALSO MY LAST!"

THE NEXT DAY IN SCHOOL,
KANE WORKED HARD, AS HIS PARENTS HAD WISHED,
AND AFTER HE ATE LUNCH
HE DREW A PEANUT BUTTER & JELLYFISH.

He drew a dog for Giulianna,
painted Weston a shark.
Kane gave them the pictures
after school in the park.

At lunchtime the next day,
the cafeteria was buzzing.
Everyone wanted a picture,
The orders came in by the dozen.

They loved the pictures so much,
they showed everyone at school.
It was at this very moment,
Kane learned a golden rule.

THE GOLDEN RULE

CREATE SOMETHING YOU'RE PROUD OF,

WITH PASSION AND SKILL.

GIVE PEOPLE WHAT THEY LOVE,

AND YOU'RE SURE TO EXCEL!

KANE PAINTED A THREE-TOED SLOTH,
AND A BIRTHDAY CAKE THAT LOOKED YUMMY,
TWO PRINCESSES FOR ISABELLA,
AND FOR BRYSON, A DANCING MUMMY!

THE ORDERS KEPT COMING IN,
AND THE MONEY DID TOO!
HE STARTED SAVING EVERY PENNY,
STASHED IN A BOX FROM HIS OLD SHOES.

He wasn't being greedy,
Kane wanted to INVEST.
His new art kit would help
make his pictures the best!

Sometimes Kane made Two Dollars,
and sometimes he made Four.
Although the money was great,
the smiles were worth so much more.

See, Kane loves what he does,
on rainy days, or when it's sunny.
The key is Happiness.
True happiness is not from money.

For My Buddy
Xander

-Kone

It started off as a hobby.
Painting pictures was his PASSION.
Kane turned his art into a business,
with custom paintings and even fashion.

KANE IMAGINES A WORLD
THAT'S COVERED IN HIS ART,
FOR ANYTHING IS POSSIBLE
IF IT COMES FROM YOUR HEART!

DALILA'S MOM HELPS HER IN THEIR GARDEN,
THEY LOVE GROWING VEGGIES AND FRUIT.
DALILA SAW AN OPPORTUNITY AND
SET UP A LOCAL DELIVERY ROUTE.

LIAM LOVES DOGGIES,
HE WOULD WALK THEM ALL DAY IF HE COULD.
HE STARTED A DOG-WALKING SERVICE
FOR ALL OF HIS NEIGHBORHOOD.

Here's some business ideas that you could do!

Skylar enjoys making bracelets
with colorful beads and twine.
She started selling them at yardsales
and now she has a shop online.

Durell had a passion for cars,
"Wash every car" was his goal.
He started a car-wash business,
and posted signs on every pole.

Interact with fellow readers!
Upload your colored photo with the hashtag
#KanesBigPicture

Interact with fellow readers!
Upload your colored photo with the hashtag
KanesBigPicture

KANE'S BIG PICTURE
BONUS
INTERACTIVE COLORING SECTION!

INTERACT WITH FELLOW READERS!
UPLOAD YOUR COLORED PHOTO WITH THE HASHTAG
#KANESBIGPICTURE

Interact with fellow readers!
Upload your colored photo with the hashtag
#KanesBigPicture

Studying *mushrooms

Robot

Interact with fellow readers!
Upload your colored photo with the hashtag
#KanesBigPicture

Interact with fellow readers!
Upload your colored photo with the hashtag
#KanesBigPicture

Interact with fellow readers!
Upload your colored photo with the hashtag
#KanesBigPicture

Kane's Big Picture

BONUS

Draw your own Picture and share with us!

Made in the USA
San Bernardino, CA
27 June 2020